ATLAS OF
THE BODY

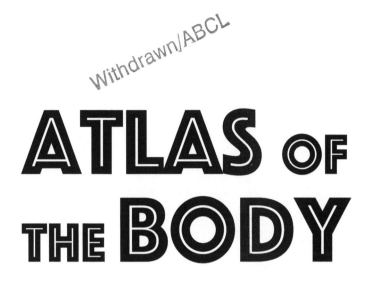

ATLAS OF THE BODY

Nicole Cuffy

Black
Lawrence
Press

Black
Lawrence
Press

www.blacklawrence.com

Executive Editor: Diane Goettel
Chapbook Editor: Kit Frick
Book and Cover Design: Amy Freels
Cover Art: "Auxilium" by Jill Capistrant. Used with permission.

Published 2018 by Black Lawrence Press.
Printed in the United States.

To Na and Thel

Contents

I. Metatarsus

On pillowy summer afternoons Maya runs to Zaire's house, watercolor sky above her scarred from passing planes. Her body is light, easy for the world to hold. She digs her toes into the hot, red earth and imagines leaping up and never coming down, but going up and up and up, burning in the white sun. Zaire waits for her on his front lawn, and he looks like a child to her, even though she is a child too. Their feet are small and hard and brown. They barely feel the ground's heat on the soles of their feet.

Damp, homey smell of the woods, dancing leaves green membranes against the sun, a private world of crystallized light and the music of birds and the small movements of unseen things. Zaire climbs a tree and Maya scrapes her knees and the insides of her thighs trying to follow him. He comes down to help her, tries to push her up, but neither of them is strong enough. They fall down, young limbs awkward and careless. Maya catches his elbow in her ribs. It does not hurt. She can smell his sweat, sour but somehow still nice, a summery smell.

Maya can dance on her toes. The uneven ground with its hidden obstacles makes it hard, but she does not mind stumbling. Zaire rises up onto his toes too, and they laugh, dancing with each other, as a part of each other. They are two wild animals. Everything in the world is their mother. They make their own music, compete with the birds. Zaire stumbles and falls, disturbs a mound of fire ants. They cover his bare feet, his bare legs, him rolling around and hollering, making Maya laugh as she screams, and him laughing and hollering, and the ants stinging. Fierce as their namesake.

...

Maya examines her hands. They are small, calloused. The backs of her hands are dry and brown, but the insides are pink, lined with brown-tinged creases. If she looks very closely, she can see her fingerprints. If she flexes all her fingers as hard as she can, she can see the green veins under her skin, the knobs of her bones. She likes the little web of skin between her thumb and her pointer finger. She likes that, no matter how hard she pinches there, it doesn't really hurt.

Maya walks to church with Zaire and his older brother. Their mothers have given them tithe money, and it jangles in their pockets, though Maya is wearing a dress with no pockets, and so her money jangles in Zaire's. 'Hey,' says Zaire's brother. 'What do you say we take this money and head to the gas station? We can get candy bars and soda.' She and Zaire look at each other. 'We're supposed to put it in the basket,' says Zaire.

Zaire's brother rolls his eyes. 'Don't be such a pussy.' She and Zaire look at each other again. They do not shrug, but the shrug is implied. What can they do? There are two of them, but still, Zaire's brother is in charge. The other day when Zaire's mom made gumbo for dinner—Maya stayed over and ate with them—Zaire's brother picked out all the chicken for himself, scooping it right off the bones and leaving only gristle and bone behind, and no one said anything to him, not even Zaire's mother.

They go to the gas station. Zaire's brother does not get soda or candy but a pack of cigarettes, and she and Zaire get a bag of extra hot Cheetos each and a Sierra Mist and a Pepsi, respectively. Among the three of them, there's eight cents left to put in the basket. They never go to church, anyway. They can't bring the food in, or else people will know where their tithing money went. They go around to the back of the gas station, where the churchgoers driving by won't see them, and she and Zaire eat their chips and drink their soda, and Zaire's brother smokes one cigarette after the other, until half the pack is gone.

II. Ascending Colon

She has only just now realized that she lives in poverty. A collection of one-eyed houses, patched with plywood, their roofs brittle and broken open in places, wounded old men. The woods she and Zaire once found so majestic are only a patch of trees that separates the houses from the weed-strangled railroad tracks. This has been her home.

She opens the refrigerator and finds a small gathering of things, none of which make a meal—pickles, a carton containing only one egg, expired milk, a half-empty jar of jelly. Zaire's refrigerator is the same. She has grown up knowing better than to complain to her mother, but she has only now realized what that means. They are not starving, but they are hungry. She is starving, though not for food. She is a trapped animal. The house smells like old books. She must get out. There is no way out. The world will push her back here, always.

Zaire's brother moved to Atlanta for two years, and now he's back home, skinny and vague, and he looks at Maya with eyes that seem to slip over her, seeing not her, but only her body. A body. Any body. 'How old are you now?' he asks, and she doesn't answer. There is something wrong with Zaire's brother, something that wasn't there before. His face is always ashy, and he has an odd smell—something like clothes that have been in a box for years and years. Zaire is not home. She escapes his brother's eyes on her body.

But her body is not her body. She is her body. She is interested in how it works. Zaire keeps telling her she will be a doctor one day. She finds him at the gas station with his friends and lures him away, promising Twix, his favorite, her treat. Zaire's brother used to hang out at the gas station. Together, she and Zaire pore over the medical textbooks they find in the library. He pulled something at basketball practice so she tries to identify the injury by the location of the hurt. She presses her fingertips to the back of his jeans-clad thigh, probing, checking the neat diagrams of muscle. Somewhere in the hamstrings. They are two explorers with nothing but a map and instinct. Biceps femoris tendinopathy. Their bodies echo each other. She can almost feel the phantom pain behind her own knee.

He holds her steady on the ladder as she returns the book to its shelf. His hand wraps around her thigh. Adductor magnus. It used to mean nothing, this kind of touch. It used to be as empty and inconsequential as a seed husk. Him touching her used to be beside the point. But now it is everything, them touching. It is full and heavy and necessary. They are both stiff. Not quite themselves anymore but actors, moving carefully as they think they should. A meticulous script, and all the while, her insides are wild, her stomach screams. They were wild animals once. She has the strangest urge to bite him, to taste him.

She is so hungry. It is not food, but everything else, the world. Zaire. Her and Zaire and the world. What she needs is not on her street with the one-eyed houses. It is not in the patch of trees she once thought was a forest. It is beyond, somewhere she can't quite imagine. She can feel her way there as she felt her way to Zaire's injury with the atlas of the body. She and Zaire walk together, their arms close but not touching, swinging in rhythm with each other, encased in an invisible, warm membrane. Their shoes are old, worn, a little too small. She knows that they are poor. I will not stay, she thinks. I will not stay.

'One day,' she says, 'we'll look back on this and it'll be like one of those sunny flashback scenes in a movie.' Zaire laughs. 'Look back on what?' he asks. 'On this,' she says. 'This moment. We'll look back and it won't be real any more. It'll be all sunny and bright, and we won't remember the smell of the trash, or how it's way too hot, or how there's chocolate stuck under your fingernails. It'll be perfect, and it'll make everything better.'

Something deep inside her belly shakes as she says this. She is taking some risk she cannot name.

For the first time, Zaire kisses her. Then they continue their walk, because the kiss was the most natural thing in the world. Since they were born, it'd been meant to happen. Maya's mouth is warm, tingling. A rush of blood to the capillaries, automatic response to a possible injury.

...

She and Zaire take the bus to Charlotte to watch the Hornets play. They have been saving for this over months, putting away all the money from their after-school jobs and supplementing those savings by selling boxes of candy bars Zaire's brother gives them. Their parents insisted that Zaire's brother go with them, but at the last minute, he said he couldn't, and she is glad of this. Now it is just her and Zaire. He is excited—he won't stop talking about how he is going to play for the Hornets one day—but she is looking out the windows, watching the trees zip by. The sun filtering through their branches is like a strobe light.

She tries pointing this out to Zaire, but he doesn't listen to her. Not really. All he can talk about right now is basketball. She doesn't care about basketball. Not really. She agreed to come with Zaire not because she's excited about the game, but because she understands his zeal. She understands that part of his intense love is his intense hate of the home they've been stuck with. His intense thirst to become unstuck. She has this same thirst. Every boy she and Zaire have grown up with has an intense love for something—basketball, football, rapping— but this love is not of that something, it is of the escape. This love is not love, it is hope.

So she never tells Zaire that even though he is good—really good—there are thousands, maybe millions, of other teenaged boys with the same dream and the same thirst. He knows this already. She hopes with him, for him. Zaire tells her that she will be a doctor one day, and she believes him. She tries to imagine how they will fit together, once all their dreams come true. It has always been so easy, fitting together. She watches the sun strobe through the trees, and eventually it hypnotizes her into sleep.

III. Umbilicus

Desperate, clawing thing, nearly impossible to move through. She'd give anything to go back home. Not the place. He'd been her home. Sharp abandonment, black over the eyes. Everything is far away; she is small, infinitesimal, nothing. Crushed under a great heel. She remembers what her child's eyes saw—it was illusion, smudges on a cave wall. Reality surprisingly harsh. She had never pictured life without him. She'd held happiness, fragile bird; she'd swallowed its feathers, spines sharp on the red, red skin of her throat. A beating in her chest, not her heart. An anti-pulse. A skeleton holding up a tapestry of flesh. Nothing is anything. White sun the other side of absolute black.

From the first shadow to stumble out of black muck, what is it we do to each other? From the crawling, stumbling, hot beginning, we have hurt. Where is this pain? Myocardium, endocardium, epicardium; left ventricle and atrium, right ventricle and atrium; epiglottis, esophagus, trachea; tunica intima, media, and adventitia, platelets, plasma, blood cells, red and white. A cancer of hurt. Metastasized. Incurable shrapnel. She hurtles forward, everything ripping away from her, bleeding behind her. He is not there anymore. He has gone. She is moving still, a reflexive twitching after decapitation.

IV. Rectus Abdominis

Her last day of residency is anticlimactic. She didn't expect a party, but the attendings she'd wanted to thank are not in their offices, the nurses she says goodbye to are lukewarm, perhaps even brisk, and it is the middle of the day. In the end, all she does is finish her paperwork and walk out the door. It is any other day. A song is stuck in her head—something old. Her mind repeats the melody over and over, but it is slippery; the lyrics are blurred, and when she focuses too hard, the whole thing slips away from her.

She meets Troy for a celebratory lunch. He is almost too happy to see her, too congratulatory. She does not know what she wants. She stares at the food on their plates, the raw carnality of it. The brutality. She is thinking of Zaire, which is strange since she has not spoken to him in almost a year, and it has been four since he broke her heart, left her for ASVEL and France. Memories of him are old scars which she sometimes traces with her fingers, remembering how they got there, how they had healed, if healing meant staying there forever but hardly ever hurting again until the very memory opened its mouth and bit.

Troy reaches across the table and takes her hand in his. Troy really loves her, she knows. What she feels for him is not quite love, she thinks, though it is close. Perhaps as close as she can get. She is so tired. Getting away, escaping the red, hot earth she grew from, had worn her out. She does not go back there. Her mother does not live there anymore, and there is nothing there for Maya. She tries to focus on Troy, his voice a deep-throated buzz. His hand is large and warm and soft. She knows what he is going to say.

She sometimes senses that three versions of her exist simultaneously. There is a version that is home with Zaire, them never hurting each other, never leaving each other. There is a version that is stringently alone, closed and efficient as a sugarcane stalk, moving through the world as through poison ivy—careful not to let anything touch her. And there is this version, here at this table of meat with Troy. Three possibilities originating from a common core of self and then moving away from each other, like the spokes in a wheel. Which is the whole one? she wonders. Which one came out unharmed?

Her fellowship is across the country. This was what she could never truly imagine as a child. She should feel more. She is detached, clinical; she is her own patient. What a patient wants is secondary to what they need. This is the best she can do. The brain's pleasure center is located along the medial forebrain bundle, a circuit of nucleus accumbens, amygdala, prefontal cortex, the ventral tegmental area. Fat and neurons and axons and dendrites and water. This is all. Just the meninges protecting the central nervous system. What if someone got through? Pierced the membranes with a pin? Could she still feel the way she is supposed to feel then? Troy presses something into her hand, small and cold.

...

She is packing and trying not to think about time. She has a picture of her grandmother as a young woman that always makes her cry because whenever she looks at that picture, she can't help but think how she knows more than the woman in that photo. She knows about the abusive first marriage, the cold second marriage, the two children, the housing project, the Virginia Slims, the swollen ankles, the tissue paper skin on the hands, the loneliness, the aborted dream of stardom, the carcinoma, the black flower on the lung that grows and grows and grows and then devours.

The woman in the photograph doesn't know any of that yet. She has hopes, dreams. She loves intensely. She believes in escape. Maya doesn't even bother looking at pictures of herself. She has no Twitter, no Instagram, and her Facebook page contains only her profile picture—a sterile portrait of her in her white lab coat, the same photo she uses for her LinkedIn page.

She does not like to think about herself the way she thinks about her grandmother, or who her grandmother used to be in that picture. She does not like to think about her position on the wheel.

She finds a box when she reaches the back of her closet. She tries to pretend to herself that she'd forgotten all about it, that she barely remembers what it is. But she has never forgotten this box. She has always been aware of its presence, whenever she opened the closet. It is the box of her things that Zaire returned to her when he left. She has never told Troy about this box, and she has never opened it. She opens it now. Before she can even see what's inside, she is overcome by the smell—it smells like cardboard and must and him. There is nothing she needs in this box. She closes it up again, takes her Sharpie, and writes in block letters that are so big they cross the gap between the flaps: TO DONATE.

V. Ilioinguinal Nerve

A sleepy familiarity, variation on a theme. Skin against skin, heat and sweat. The palms of their hands, their fingertips. Skin a conduit of fervor. Their own private biology. Chemistry, an alchemy. Collision of matter. This is older than them. He kisses the small scars on the insides of her knees. Only he can see them; he was there when she got them. His bony, almost feminine wrists. His veins reach for hers; she can see them, embossed on him, abstract art. For him, it's the feel of her; her softness, her smallness. His mouth opens against hers and their breathing becomes the tangled vines in a jungle. For her, it's the smell of him. Deep and hers. Variations on a theme: tender, demanding, hungry, ungentle, careful, tentative, sure.

They feel each other realizing they fit together, not as puzzle pieces, but as ligament to bone. It curls up from between them, a phoenix. Neither of them saying it, but both of them thinking it. The words are imprisoned in their throats, but they make themselves known, through the brush of the fingers, refrain of lips, foreheads resting together, the breath together, the pulse together, the two of them an abyss. The words are infinitely there, in the abyss. Horror of love. It makes itself known. It echoes into infinity.

VI. Cephalic Vein

It might be that you never existed. Or that you are hiding. I will make you hiding. You never thought about time, or its casual atrocities. Your teeth bright shells in the light. You smile and an infinite number of things happen at once. An unknowable number of small movements, the world shifting around us, in us. Hear me, in your eyes and in your bones, a pinpoint into the cavities of your sinuses. You press the sunflower seed into my tongue. I taste its salt and yours.

Imagine this great firmament: Can you breathe? Do you remember the first time you touched me and knew you were touching me? Do you remember the last day? You stood in your coat and a great murder of crows plumed out behind you. Black wings. A chaos lesser than the chaos of pain. Why did you cry? I do not cry but howl. I hide from you, and you hide from me until we are both lost. You are a wild animal. You have made a savage out of me. You drew me a picture of a heart. Anatomically correct. With the colored pencils you never let anyone see you use anymore. No one but me. You bare your teeth a little as you concentrate, pink hint of your tongue. The left pulmonary arteries dwarf the aorta, the atriums small as pebbles. You would die if you had this heart. I tape it to the inside of *Gray's Anatomy*.

Look at time. Do you remember the fire ants? Do you remember how you howled?

VII. Parietal Bone

Today, she hears the news that Zaire's brother is dead. It happens after she leaves work, while she's making a stop at McDonald's on her way home, not because she likes the food—in fact, she hates it—but because it is the only place around where she can get food at this late hour, and she hasn't eaten since the vegan granola bar she stole from an intern at lunch. There was a fire at a local housing project that got out of control, and she's been engaged all day in the Sisyphean task of keeping people alive who ought to have died. She wasn't able to save everyone.

Though she didn't grow up in a housing project, she grew up in the same kind of poverty as the people she's been treating, and so, all day, she's been thinking of home, and thinking that it could've been her who'd burned up in a fire started by some kid playing with matches on a patched-up couch. She's been thinking that there's no such thing as fair, and that she and Zaire are the only people she knew who got the break everyone's dreaming about, but at what cost?

She pulls into the dark McDonald's parking lot, turns off the engine, but does not get out of the car. She sits in the stillness. If someone were to ask her right now why she does not leave her car, she would not know what to say. In fact, she asks herself this question in her head, and she has no answer. All she knows is that her legs are not ready to move, her body is not ready to be out in the open air.

She takes out her cell phone and performs her reflexive circuit of apps—Gmail, The Weather Channel, and Simple. She has an impulse to check the local news from home, so she opens Safari, finds the local new station's website, and skims the headlines. "Cribs Recalled for Collapse Hazard"; "Drunk Driver Crashes into Local Walgreens"; "4-Star Receiver Turns to Basketball Next"; "The Methamphetamine Epidemic: What you need to know"; "Local woman wears red all day every day. Here's why"; "Man's Body Discovered Outside of Bethel AME Has Been Identified."

The last one catches her interest, in part due to its poor syntax, and she clicks on the link. The first photo is a grainy shot of a dilapidated church. The second photo is a mug shot. It is Zaire's brother. He is older in the picture, but still recognizable. She reads the article. The cause of death is still being determined. The family is not mentioned, but the pastor of the church makes a statement: Our prayers are with the deceased and his family.

She has a strange feeling, like being told something would hurt and then being surprised at the pain. She is not exactly surprised, but she is sad, crestfallen. She wonders about Zaire and his mother. They're so far away from her now. This feels personal, but it's not, not anymore. She hasn't seen Zaire's brother since she was in high school, had never even particularly liked him, and yet it feels as though her own brother has died. Or rather, it feels as though an old, vestigial part of her is gone. Like her gallbladder has been removed.

She sits in her car for a while longer, unsure of what to do. She is unsteady, regressed. She thinks about calling her mother but then remembers the time. Something black flicks across the sky in front of her. It is either a bat or a bird. She opens the car door and steps outside. It is not nearly as cold as she'd thought.

...

Maya goes out for a walk alone. She walks until she finds quiet, and loses the endless babbling of people, a brook of syllables and breath and inflection—the things that make a language. She walks into silence. This part of the country is still unfamiliar to her. There are woods here, real woods. She walks

surrounded and alone. She has taken her wedding and engage-
ment rings off, put them in a shallow pocket in her sweatshirt.
It is as close to naked as she can be here. She trips over a large,
fallen branch and the rings tumble out, rolling toward the base
of a growing fern. She watches and bends to retrieve them.

She finds there a baby bird, gummy pink skin, half-closed eyes
the color of a bruise, nubby, underdeveloped wings, shimmer
of rudimentary feathers. She leans closer, holding her breath.
It is alive; she can see the rapid rise and fall of its small chest.
She has heard that it is best not to interfere with nature, but
she is a doctor, and death is a longtime adversary of hers. She
picks up the small bird. It makes an awkward protest with its
meager wings. A weak, damp brush against the base of her
thumb. She cups the bird in her hands to keep it warm and
straightens, begins to look for a nest.

The problem is that there is birdsong everywhere. Cathedral of
music and green filtered light. The bird has stopped struggling
in her hands. She opens them a little, sees the barely feathered
chest continuing to rise and fall, impossibly fast. Sharp chirps
sound near her. Sawing alarm call of a chickadee. The nest is
right above her, mostly hidden in a mossy cavity in the tree.
She can see the fibers of it just showing. She cannot reach
it—she will have to stand on a protruding root and climb a bit.
Carefully, she tucks the bird into her shirt. It squirms in the
space between her breasts.

She steps up onto the root, waits until she has her balance
before reaching for a low nub on which to pull herself up. Zaire

used to make this look so effortless. She stands on the very tips of her toes and pulls, her feet coming up, pain of effort in her arms and abdomen. She hoists herself up until she can rest her feet on the branches and look down into the nest. The mother is there, and three other pink babies. The mother hisses—primal, Jurassic warning—and puffs up, jabbing the side of the nest with her beak. The babies screech. Gently, she takes the bird out of her shirt. Its mouth is wide, a great red opening into the void of its guts. Keeping her fingers and the baby away from the mother's beak, she puts the baby bird in its nest, watches for a moment or two to make sure it's secure, that its mother won't eject it, and she hops down from the tree. She wasn't even very high up. Her knees quake slightly at her landing.

She'd once watched the dissection of a bird. Its insides small and fragile. When she dissected her first cadaver she saw the similarities, the same fragility, the implausibility of life. She wondered what one would find now, if they dissected her. She couldn't imagine the network of organs and blood vessels and muscle. Not in herself. A landscape instead. Vast plane, illogical dance of darkness and light, below, a complex geometry of twisted things, and above, a void. Voids, deeper and deeper. Craters of loss. In fact, loss is the only language of life. One day, the body too will be lost, and then there is nothing to dissect anymore.

Nicole Cuffy is a proud Brooklyn emigrant who enjoys yoga, ballet, and writing literary fiction. Her work can be found in *Mason's Road* and *The Masters Review Volume VI*. Nicole holds a BA in Writing from Columbia University and an MFA in Fiction from the New School. She does her best writing when she's writing by hand, and she is a high-functioning book addict. When she isn't reading, writing, or yogaing, she is most likely dancing. She can be found muddling her way through Twitter and life in general @nicolethecuffy.